THE SEASONAIRES

JANNA KING

PEGASUS BOOKS

NEW YORK LONDON

THE SEASONAIRES

Pegasus Books, Ltd.
148 W 37th Street, 13th Floor
New York, NY 10018

First Pegasus Books edition May 2018

Interior design by Maria Fernandez

Library of Congress Cataloging-in-Publication Data is available.

ISBN: 978-1-68177-739-9

10 9 8 7 6 5 4 3 2 1

Printed in the United States of America
Distributed by W. W. Norton & Company
www.pegasusbooks.us

For Izzy and Jake—my life.

PROLOGUE

July 4th

Mia could see the shapes of revelers sitting on the dark beach. Their conversations were swallowed by the fireworks over Nantucket Harbor, the sea grass and yards of sand. She turned inland and flashed a bright smile as a red, white, and blue burst fanned out behind her. She dropped the smile, glanced at the selfie, and captioned it:

Happy 4th! #BeWyld #seasonaire
#dreamsummer #fireworks

As she pressed the "+" icon on the Instagram Story screen to post, the phone was smacked from her hand. It skipped off the concrete deck into the pool. She turned to see Presley's face, furrowed in anger.

"What the fuck, Mia?" snapped Presley. The word "fuck" sounded wrong in her lilting Georgia Peach accent.

"Lyndon'll be pissed if we don't post," Mia replied.

"And if we *do*, everyone'll know we were here. That's worse."

"It was just my face and some fireworks. No one could tell where I am." Mia fished out the phone before it sank. "Besides, you knocked it out of my hand before I posted."

She showed the phone to Presley, screen black, water bubbling beneath the cracked glass. "Now it's broken."

"Good," said Presley.

Their attention turned again to the middle of the pool. The lifeless body was floating, face down, arms and legs splayed out like a golden starfish.

"He *did* have a nice ass." Presley cocked her head. "But he was a damn dog, hounding nonstop. Didn't understand the word 'no.'"

"Fuuuuuuck," muttered Mia, crouching down, knees weak and hands shaking. She swallowed the swell of tears, knowing that if she released them, she wouldn't stop.

Another blast of fireworks made her jump, despite the thumping house music echoing from the estate empty of revelers. The bassline met the hard beat of Mia's heart as she watched the blood turn the pool's crystal surface to tie-dye, like the shirts she used to make at Y summer camp a decade ago. Tie-dye was the start of Mia's obsession with fashion. Now she represented Lyndon Wyld, one of the world's hottest clothing lines, spending a dream summer in Nantucket as a seasonaire for the brand. It was all expenses paid as long as she shared every moment with her Instagram and Snapchat followers.

But Presley was right. This wasn't a moment for sharing. Mia's mind raced. *I should've gone with Jade.* Jade's dad's annual Blue Bash at his Hamptons mansion was in full swing. It was widely known that every celebrity on earth was there, but as far Mia knew, no dead bodies.

She couldn't look away, as much as she wanted to. She had never seen a dead body before. The closest thing was her mother, who had grown so sick, pale, and gaunt, her frail bones were just a hanger for her tissue-paper skin. She was fading away. But she hadn't been . . . killed.

"Get your tiny ass in *here*," Presley demanded, breaking Mia's trance. She took long strides toward the pool house that flickered with light from the candles burning inside. Mia followed past the flagpole, where the red Wear National flag fluttered beneath Old Glory. She stepped over plastic cups, cigarette butts, and soggy potato chips. Shaking, she wrapped her cardigan around her sundress even though the night air was warm.

When Mia crossed the threshold of the open door she stopped in her tracks. Ruby was lying on the red-and-white-striped daybed, unclothed and unconscious, her right eyelid swollen to twice its normal size.

"Oh my God, Ruby!" she cried.

The septum ring in Ruby's nose was covered in blood. Blood was also smeared across her face.

"As if that bullring wasn't fug enough." Presley scowled. Save for her earlobes, Presley's flawless body was void of piercings and tattoos. Mia had one tat, a small sunflower just above her ankle. Ruby had too many to count.

Woven bracelets and a thin blue enamel bangle hung from her limp wrist. Next to her hand, with its chipped silver polish, was a Smith & Wesson revolver in matching gun-metal.

Overwhelmed, Mia's stomach roiled and forced out its contents.

Presley pulled a makeup compact from her purse, opened it, and held the mirror to Ruby's mouth. She looked and saw faint breath fog. "He messed her up, but she's alive."

Mia released a sob, then lifted a plush white towel from the ground. She moved to lay it over Ruby's naked body.

"Don't," ordered Presley.

"She's just so . . ."

"It's better if they find her like this. Doesn't take a law degree to see it was self-defense," said Presley.

"This is insane." Mia's eyes were glued to Ruby as if she could, like a magician, will her to be okay. "I can't believe anyone would do this."

Presley just shrugged.

"What the hell, Presley?" Mia motioned to Ruby.

Presley waved a hand. "I shouldn't dis the girl in her current state, but she makes my trailer park cousins look like royals."

A smartphone on the floor buzzed. Presley picked it up. The screen's wallpaper was a selfie of Ruby in a tiny bikini covered with Wear National logos, her long blond hair with violet streaks blowing in the beach breeze.

"But you were right about *this*." Presley turned the phone around to show Mia a text from Mac:

Are u ok?

"She was for sure buying drugs from him. They were probably fucking, too."

Presley grabbed the towel from Mia and wiped the phone before she let it drop to the floor. "Regardless, any scumbag who would do this to a woman deserves what he gets."

"Why were you here anyway?" asked Mia. "You'd eat dirt before going to a Wear National party."

"I thought Mac was here, bringing a keg from the bar. I came to apologize to him because I was being a first-class cunt." She nodded to Ruby's smartphone. "But now I know my cuntiness was warranted. He wasn't here, but—"

"Enough with the soap opera shit, Presley!" Mia exploded. "We need to call nine-one-one!"

"Whoa!" Presley leaned away. "I was going to do that, sugar, when *you* arrived." Presley lifted the wall phone receiver.

The fireworks finale started outside with a steady stream of pops, bangs, and booms. Presley and Mia froze, waiting for silence. After the finale ended, Presley dialed.

The operator's voice rose from the receiver. "Nine-one-one. What's the emergency?" Presley hung up, wiping the phone with the towel.

Mia glared at her. "What? Why would you hang up?"

"They'll come. Caller ID."

Presley mopped up Mia's vomit with the towel and saw a tiny diamond-tipped coke spoon in the corner. "That's pretty, but I'll leave it."

Mia's dismay turned to disgust when Presley shoved the balled-up barf towel at her. "Your hurl, girl." Presley grabbed her arm and strode toward the door.

Mia resisted. "What are you doing?"

"*We* are leaving," said Presley. "The fireworks are over. The other brand sluts will be back soon."

"We can't leave!" said Mia.

"We called nine-one-one, we did our job. But I didn't sign up for this. Did you?" Presley's arms were spread wide, as if presenting the scene to Mia.

Mia took a long last look at Ruby, then walked out the door with Presley. *No, she didn't sign up for this.*

ONE

Memorial Day Weekend

M y suitcase is way too small," grumbled Mia as she sat on a large piece of luggage.

"Move over, lil sis."

Mia slid right and her only brother, Sean, sat next to her on the suitcase. She reached underneath and pushed a couple skirts and shirts into the opening. She had watched every BuzzFeed video on packing hacks, but rolling sweaters and sticking underwear in her shoes didn't help.

"Lose either the boots or the sewing kit," said Sean.

Mia nodded to the old sewing machine on her desk. "I'd fit *that* in here if I could." Grunting, she zipped around the suitcase's perimeter. She stood and brushed her hands together, grinning triumphantly. "Didn't have to lose anything."

Sean chuckled. "You're pretty cocky for someone who's never been out of Southie."

"We visited Dad once in Paramus." Mia picked up a satin jewelry pouch from the nightstand, dropping in four thin blue enamel bangle bracelets that had been sitting next to a framed photo of a younger Mia and Sean with their mom, Kathryn, a radiant brunette with sparkling green eyes. There were no photos of her dad anywhere in this small bedroom. Ray, a handsome job- less bullshitter, had cheated on Kathryn countless times. When Mia was six, her parents split and Ray left South Boston. Mia saw him once a year around the holidays, when he visited from New Jersey, where he lived with his new wife and two kids. She didn't know what her half siblings looked like, which was fine with her. When she was ten, Ray gave her twenty bucks for Christmas, but made such a big deal out of it that she vowed she would never take another handout. She'd forge her own way and take care of her mom, who had devoted her life to Mia and Sean.

Kathryn worked at the Gillette factory during the day, coming home to make dinner and help with homework. Then, she got up at 3:00 a.m. and went to work at the neighborhood bakery, preparing treats for the morning customers. When she woke Mia and Sean for school, she smelled like a vanilla cupcake.

Four years ago, Kathryn got tired, *really* tired. She thought it was because she ran herself ragged, but after another year, when she could barely get out of bed, she finally went to the doctor. She was diagnosed with non-Hodgkin's lymphoma. Mia's part- time job at a neighborhood thrift shop helped pick up the slack. When Sean wasn't at school, he worked at McGoo's Pizza. They were hanging on in their little apartment, but barely.

One February afternoon, Mia was arranging merchandise at the thrift shop. The snowy weather wasn't ideal for shopping, so the store was empty, save for Mia's boss, Pam. Pam spent most of her time taking selfies, since Mia had proven she was good at making a sale. A pretty thirty-something entered and started browsing, one eye on Mia. Mia noticed her put-together winter outfit, which included an Hermès bag, a chic felt fedora over her long blond hair, and a sapphire solitaire necklace around her neck. She was a different type of clientele than the usual neighborhood women who visited in a chatty clump.

Mia picked a piece of lint off a magenta silk top she was straightening on a hanger. "Can I help you?"

The woman touched the silk top. "My Lyndon Wyld tweed trousers would look brilliant with this," she said in a British accent.

"I love Lyndon Wyld," Mia replied.

"I could've called that when I walked in here."

"But those clothes are a little pricey for me, and they never end up here because people hang on to them like gold."

"That's true," said the woman. "But they don't cost a penny for seasonaires."

"For who?" Mia shifted under the woman's gaze.

"Lyndon Wyld chooses six brand ambassadors to go to Nantucket for the summer."

"Nantucket? I've never been lucky enough to visit. Come to think of it, I don't know anyone who has." Mia continued to straighten the racks.

The woman smiled. "Seasonaires party, loll in the sun, wear great clothes, and get paid twenty grand to do it."

"Sounds too good to be true. Where do I sign up?" Mia said, still only half paying attention.

"The application is on the website. You have to make a video. Just be you, because your style is the dog's bollocks."

Mia offered a perplexed chuckle.

"That means 'fabulous.'" The woman motioned to Mia's ensemble. "Classic with just a hint of edge."

"Thanks." Mia glanced down at herself. "All gently loved. Mom's turtleneck, boots are from here, and these"—she smoothed her high-waisted jeans—"were my friend's. She gained the Freshman Fifteen and now they're mine."

The woman clapped her hands once. "Her gain was your gain."

Mia wanted to say that she would've gladly gained the Freshman Fifteen all her girlfriends loathed. They got to go to college. She had applied to MassArt for fashion design, but the steep tuition tanked her plans, even with financial aid. During what would have been her freshman and sophomore years, she'd taught herself everything: how to draw designs, make patterns, sew by hand and machine. She needed to get out of Southie, and fashion would be her ticket.

The woman pointed to the silver framed cutouts at the ankles of Mia's jeans. "I *lust* the grommets."

"I added those," said Mia.

"Smashing!" The woman leaned in and whispered, "I know people, so I'll nudge if you throw in that fab scarf with the top." She nodded to a paisley scarf hanging on a nearby hook.

Mia's boss was busy taking selfies in berets, so Mia slipped the scarf in a bag with the top and rang up the sale.

That weekend, Mia went on the Lyndon Wyld website. Sean helped Mia make a video. He manned her smartphone camera while she went about "Favorite Activities," as the website instructed. She sketched and stitched lace into a vintage blouse, talking about how she had been lucky enough to inherit her grandmother's sewing machine. She cooked pasta, made snow angels, and revealed her obsession with documentaries. South Boston's beaches were nearby, but Mia's fair, slightly freckled skin had never seen a day there, so she chuckled when she said she'd need "a boatload of sunscreen" for eight weeks in Nantucket.

At the end of the video, she and her mother kissed toward the camera. Kathryn's sparkling eyes were the only feature that remained from the photo on Mia's nightstand. Cancer had robbed her of her radiance.

"Way to tug at the heartstrings," Sean said sarcastically as he transferred the video to Mia's laptop.

"Why are you being a dick?" Mia shot back. "You've had fun every friggin' day playing baseball while you work toward *your* dream. I should get a chance at mine." Sean had received a full baseball scholarship at Boston College, and the majors were already recruiting him.

Mia pointed to the Lyndon Wyld site with its bold headline beneath a slideshow of catalog-perfect bodies and smiling faces doing everything the blond woman at the thrift shop described:

A seasonaire's summer is the dream of a lifetime! #BeWyld

"I get it, Mia." Sean looked at her with empathy. "I just think that showing Mom is a little . . . manipulative."

"I'm supposed to share my life," Mia replied. "Mom *is* my life."

Before uploading the video, Mia filled out the online application. Sean noticed the age requirement: *21–24.*

"Well, *that* sucks," said Sean.

Mia keyed in *21.*

"What are you doing?" Sean furrowed his brow. "You're not twenty-one for another ten months."

"We need the money, right?"

Sean couldn't argue—they *did* need the money.

They read the release form: *Participant assumes all risks, to include, without limitation, serious injury, illness or disease, death and/or property damage.*

"Because lounging on the beach in trendy clothes is dangerous," scoffed Sean.

"They're covering their asses." Mia clicked the form's *Accept* box, thinking, *What's the worst thing that could happen?*

The e-mail came in April. Mia shrieked, then danced around her room like a goofball. She ran to the liquor store down the street for a bottle of sparkling apple cider to celebrate with her family. She bought a box of crackers and placed them next to the homeless woman sleeping against the dull brick building next to hers. Most of the buildings on her block were dull and brick. Parts of South Boston were changing with an influx of upwardly-mobile hipsters, but until this e-mail, she feared life would never change for her.

Sean texted that he was taking an extra shift at work, so Mia and Kathryn toasted alone.

A check for half her seasonaire's fee arrived a month later, with the rest coming at the job's end. She stared at it for ten solid minutes because she'd never seen that many zeros in real life. She deposited it in the household account.

"Use the debit card to buy whatever you want there," Kathryn said as she swallowed her meds at the kitchen table with Sean.

"How about a yacht?" Mia put the spaghetti she'd cooked on plates. "That's what Nantucketers buy, right?"

"Don't say 'Nantucketers' or you might end up at the bottom of the Sound." Sean sprinkled Parmesan cheese on his spaghetti and dug in.

"Bite your tongue, Sean." Kathryn gave his hand a play-slap, then looked at Mia. "I know you'll be careful."

Memorial Day couldn't come soon enough. Sean pretended he didn't give a shit that Mia was leaving, but he ended up pulling her in for a bear hug.

"Bye, turd," he said. "Have a really terrible time."

Mia laughed, tears welling for a beat.

"Don't do anything I wouldn't do," said Kathryn. She had been pretty wild at Mia's age—that's how she'd ended up with Sean. She took Mia's face in her hands and kissed her forehead, her cheeks, and her nose, like she had when Mia was little.

"Mom," Mia chuckled.

Mia took the bus to the Hyannis harbor terminal. She stared out the window for the entire ninety-minute drive, because she was afraid if she spoke to anyone she would burst into tears. She felt guilty for leaving her mom and even guiltier for saddling Sean with all the responsibility.

At the harbor, she stepped onto the ferry and walked through to the bow, passing parents putting life jackets on excited children, their bored teenagers texting. Mia imagined that the couples with their arms around each other were heading for a romantic getaway. The few people near her age were already drinking beers and joking around before the boat even set off.

Mia's guilt seemed to wash away in the wake as she floated farther and farther from Southie. She took a photo of the calm waters and clear blue skies ahead, posting to her Instagram account, miamamasgrl:

Here's to the dream. #BeWyld #summer

TWO

"I will end that fucking rodent for biting off me," snapped Lyndon into her smartphone, which she gripped with meticulously French-manicured fingers.

The young male flight attendant approached and placed down a tea setting—fine china, engraved with the Lyndon Wyld logo, which also adorned the green and beige seats on the private jet. Lyndon lifted the teapot lid, then lowered the phone to her side.

"It's not hot enough, I can tell," she said in her clipped British accent.

"I apologize, Ms. Wyld." The flight attendant picked up the tray.

"Thank you," added Lyndon with a smile that said, *I value you, but I own you, too.*

The flight attendant returned to the galley and Lyndon went back to her phone call. "Did you just dare say to me 'Imitation is the best form of flattery?'" Her smile had turned to a glower. "Tell

Otto Hahn that if I see one item—one fucking sock or headband or pair of knickers—that looks remotely like mine, I will sue him so fast, his tiny todger will fall off."

She clicked off the phone and swiftly exhaled.

Grace, Lyndon's younger sister and personal assistant, reached into her tote for a gold pillbox. She handed Lyndon a Valium.

Lyndon swallowed the pill with a sip of water from the logo-adorned bottle Grace held toward her. "As if it's not bad enough that he opened a Wear National store down the street from ours, he's also calling his paltry band of brand ambassadors *seasonaires.*"

"What did Elaine say about that?" asked Grace.

"You mean the idiot who calls herself my attorney? She said I don't have a lock on the name."

"We'll find a new attorney." Grace shrugged. "I can't fart without hitting one waiting to be your counsel."

"Poor things." Lyndon grimaced. "I shared a room with you growing up, remember?"

"If you can't toot in front of your sister, who can you toot in front of?"

"Attorneys, apparently."

Grace broke into a laugh, which loosened up Lyndon. She chuckled.

When Lyndon and Grace were young and poor, which was the case over two decades earlier, they worked at a posh resort in the Cotswolds. They pined over the clothes that their wealthier peers wore. Grace lamented that "everyone should be able to look that toff." Lyndon, never one to play victim, took that idea and ran with it. She zipped through a fast-track undergraduate business degree at Staffordshire University, but learned the most rising through the ranks working at Selfridges department store. The result was her self-named clothing line.

Now, on the cusp of forty, Lyndon looked closer to thirty thanks to some strategic nips, tucks, and injections. With her smooth golden bob and Pilates-toned body, she was impeccably classic, yet accessible-by-design. That's why her line was impeccably classic, yet accessible-by-design. Lyndon had always been the beauty and the brains. Grace, a curvy ginger, was the humor and the help, following behind her older sister because she didn't have the drive or focus to steer her own ship.

Grace opened her laptop. "Forget about Otto's manky little tarts. Let's review our picks for this summer since we're going to meet them shortly." She clicked on the file: *Seasonaires*. "Fresh meat!"

This elicited a chuckle from Lyndon. "Don't be wretched, Grace!"

Lyndon paid homage to her salad days working at the resort by calling her brand ambassadors "seasonaires." They came and went with the vacation seasons—summers in coveted locales like Martha's Vineyard, Cape Cod, and Ibiza; winters in Aspen, Gstaad, and the French Alps. Her first crew of trendsetters converged on Nantucket eight years earlier, and after that summer, her brand's margins exploded.

Six sub-folders opened on Grace's laptop screen: Grace clicked on the one marked "Cole" to reveal a photo of a handsome twenty-something with emerald green eyes and a gentle smile.

"I still don't understand why you wanted this lad," said Grace. "He's got the look, but no social following."

"People appear out of nowhere and succeed," replied Lyndon. "Look at Otto. I was already busting my arse for years when he popped out of his hovel." She pointed to Mia's folder. "Remind me about this pretty bird."

Grace opened the folder. "Mia from Boston." She played the video without the sound. "She's the one with the sick mum."

"Right, right," said Lyndon. "We should bring the mum out for a weekend. Put her up at The Wauwinet with a butler. Take her on the yacht, get her a massage, have the girl snap and post the whole thing. We'll look like bloody heroes."

Lyndon's phone buzzed with an Instagram notification:

thenewpresley just posted a video

She clicked on the notification and a video played. Freshly made-up, long corn silk–hued hair curled to beach-sexy perfection, Presley stood in front of the Lyndon Wyld Nantucket store. "I'm baaaack, y'all!" she drawled. "This summer is going to be wild. Lyndon Wyld, that is!"

The video ended. "Our reigning queen just hit nine hundred and thirty thousand followers," said Lyndon.

"Your idea to bring her back was brilliant," remarked Grace.

"And your scrappy Southie is positively ace." Lyndon nodded to Mia in her video. "A little healthy competition never hurt anyone."

THREE

Despite the full ferry, the ride was the most peaceful two hours Mia could remember. Hundreds of sailboats were a white tufted welcome into Nantucket Harbor, skimming the water like a choreographed dance.

A man with his arms around a woman pointed to the sea of boats. "Figawi weekend is the start of Nantucket's summer season," Mia overheard him say.

"Figawi?" The woman glanced back at him.

"In 1972, when three drunk friends in a sailing race here got lost in the fog, one shouted in his thick New England accent 'Where the fuck aw we?' Figawi."

The woman laughed. Mia chuckled to herself.

The ferry was close enough that she could see the detail on the matching white, gray, and brown wood-shingled homes and